Tapestries of Freedom
Jason's Journey Through Time

Dr. William Clifton Green II

ABSOLUTE AUTHOR PUBLISHING HOUSE

Publisher: Absolute Author Publishing House
Editor: Dr. Melissa Caudle

Hardback ISBN: 978-1-64953-974-8
Paperback ISBN: 978-1-64953-975-5
eBook ISBN: 978-1-64953-976-2

Dedication

I dedicate this book to those who persist. This is my whisper to you across space and time.

Table of Contents

Chapter 1

Echoes Through Time

The year was 2121. Ancient neon lights bled into the artificial twilight, painting the cityscape in hues of futuristic dreams hinting of echoes of a long-ago past time. Jason, a young man with eyes heavy with the weight of time, sought to reconnect with the distant past. He held the latest device in his hands, pulsing with the energy of time manipulation. Emanating from this device was the legacy of a forgotten ancestor who dared to dream of rewriting the wrongs of the past.

Jason wasn't a soldier nor a scholar but a historian, haunted by the echoes of a forgotten era. The year 1850, a time etched in blood and stained with injustice, called to him from the dusty pages of history books archived in online journals and so profoundly felt by the device he held. Through the device, he could see and feel everything, and he knew the fate of his forgotten ancestor. However, the technology his people possessed whispered promises of a world where freedom could be made possible by any means.

His journey began not with a fanfare of trumpets but with the quiet hum of the temporal engine, a machine that defied the very fabric of time. With a jolt that rattled his bones and a dizzying blur of colors, Jason thrust into the heart of his chosen year, landing unceremoniously in a field of cotton, the lingering smell of the time travel machine intermingling with the sunbaked earth filling his lungs.

He was an enigma, to be sure, a man from a world of technical innovation, sleek metals, and chrome who suddenly found himself in a landscape of wood and iron. His sleek, synthetic clothes screamed of the future, a stark contrast to the rough-spun tunics and calloused hands of the farmers who eyed him with suspicion as he walked. The air vibrated with the unfamiliar rhythm of horseshoes against dirt roads and the rhythmic clang of hammers shaping steel.

He stumbled into the heart of Meadowbrook, a quaint village untouched by the winds of change. The landscape was clean, and the air was pure and in perfect harmony, but beneath the surface of this world and timeline, he saw the scars of a nation divided, the echoes of a conflict yet to come. The opulent mansion of Blackwood Plantation loomed on the horizon, a monument to centuries of stolen lives, dreams yet draped in whispered promises of rebellion and redemption.

The memory of Sarah, a tapestry woven from the threads of her future suffering, burned bright in his mind. He knew her story, a tale of resilience and brutality, not from forgotten online archives but from her raw emotions he had downloaded into his neural implant. Her pain, his chosen anchor in this past, fueled his resolve. He couldn't technically rewrite history in his timeline, but he could become a witness, a guardian angel in a world teetering on the brink. Perhaps he could create a timeline where humanity could march in unison toward the industrial era. If this could be achieved, then the human race might, in this timeline, reach the singularity in the early 1900s or sooner.

As twilight painted the sky in shades of dying embers, Jason stood at the edge of his new reality, his heart heavy with the burden of the all-encompassing knowledge from his devices and implant. His mind burned with the fire of his noble purpose. He was a man from outside this time, a historian turned warrior, ready to step into the shadows of the past and fight for a future where freedom wasn't just a deferred dream languishing in the wind but a promise guaranteed by the echoes of time.

Chapter 2

Whispers in the Wind

The rooster's crow awakened Jason from a restless sleep. The creaking of the floorboards in the inn room, the odd smells here and there, and the sound of the wind bearing down on thin branches all took their toll. He hadn't slept peacefully since arriving in 1850, haunted by Sarah's story and the weight of his mission.

Breakfast was a bland affair of coarse bread, and watery porridge served along with lukewarm milk that tasted faintly of metal and other impurities common. His stomach protested these unfamiliar tastes. His devices had microscope applications that could identify the number of impurities in the food and drink. His mind was elsewhere, however. He needed information, a way to connect with Sarah before her life took the tragic turn, he knew all too well.

He ventured out into the dusty streets of Meadowbrook, the summer sun already relentlessly scorching the earth. The humidity had reached the tipping point, albeit in a pre-global warming manner, not as bad as in the twenty-first century, according to his devices. The villagers eyed him with curiosity and disdain, his polished clothes and something of what seemed to be a northern, non-rhotic accent of the future clashing with their rough attire and drawling speech. His neural implant, tucked beneath his hair, thrummed with its silent archive, a constant reminder of the future he'd left behind. The implant helped him adapt quickly to the social situation. He began to talk, and act like them.

He sought the tavern, a low-lit den buzzing with the murmurs of men and the clinking of glasses. It was a den of secrets, a place where gossip flowed like cheap ale. He ordered a drink, the whiskey burning his throat with unaccustomed fire. "Looking for something, stranger?" rasped a voice beside him.

It was an old man, his face etched with the lines of a life lived under the southern sun. Jason recognized him from his historical research – Silas, the overseer of Blackwood Plantation, the man who would inflict unimaginable suffering on Sarah.

A wave of rage and disgust washed over him, but he choked it down, remembering his mission. He chugged the glass of whiskey and turned toward Silas. "Just passing through now," he lied, forcing a smile. "Been hearin' good things about the local brew."

Silas eyed him shrewdly, a flicker of suspicion in his eyes. "Heard good things about you too, city feller. Folks been talking. Say you come from places beyond our wildest dreams."

Jason's heart hammered against his ribs. This was his chance. "Maybe I have," he admitted, keeping his voice low. "Maybe I know things… things about the future."

Silas leaned closer, his breath reeking of tobacco and local brew. "What kinds of things? Can you tell me… about fortune? About change?"

Jason recognized his opportunity. He knew Blackwood was struggling financially, their cotton yield dwindling.

He spun a tale of technological advancements, new markets, and bountiful harvests just beyond their grasp. Silas listened, his eyes gleamed with avarice and hope.

"I can't give you answers," Jason said finally, "but I can show you the path. If you're willing to listen."

A sly smile spread across Silas's face. "Lead the way, city feller. Let's see what this future of yours holds."

As Jason followed Silas out of the tavern, the sun had climbed high in the sky, casting long shadows that seemed to dance with the secrets of Jason's possessions. He knew he was playing a dangerous game, walking a tightrope between manipulating the past and protecting Sarah, but he would take the risk for her, for the chance to rewrite her destiny.

Word of Jason's "future knowledge" spread like wildfire through Meadowbrook. Soon, farmers and merchants crowded around him, seeking glimpses of their fortune in his eyes. He played the role of a prophet, weaving tales of prosperity and change while subtly pushing them toward a path of economic independence, a path that would weaken the hold of Blackwood on their lives. He had ideas, inventions, and even played the Shaman, giving medicines to the locals, which saved lives.

Meanwhile, he kept a close eye on the plantation, searching for a glimpse of Sarah. He saw her working in the fields, her back bent under the weight of cotton, her spirit dimmed but not extinguished. Each day, the urge to intervene, to pull her away from the path of suffering, grew more assertive. He knew he couldn't act rashly. One wrong move could tip the delicate balance he had established, throwing both Sarah and him into even greater danger. He had to bide his time, to gain their trust, to wait for the right moment to act.

As the sun dipped below the horizon, casting long shadows across the fields, Jason knew his time was running out. The whispers in the wind grew louder, carrying the scent of impending danger. He had set the wheels in motion, but the fight for Sarah, for freedom, had just begun.

Chapter 3

Embers of the Inferno

The fire in the slave quarters wasn't just a flicker of defiance; it was a bonfire reflecting in Sarah's eyes, burning like a promise whispered through time. Jason cloaked in the shroud of the woods, felt the heat stab at his soul, a testament to the storm he'd helped brew. Whispers of freedom had blossomed into shouts, the rhythmic clang of pots morphing into the drumbeat of rebellion.

He couldn't be seen, not yet. His role was that of a puppeteer, pulling strings from the shadows, ensuring the play reached its unseen climax. He was a ghost in the anachronistic machine, manipulating Silas' greed for future harvests like a puppeteer's thread. All the while, Silas was oblivious to the seeds of revolution sown within his cotton fields.

His heart pounded a different rhythm, a frantic counterpoint to the drums. He had a vision. Sarah, the firebrand at the heart of the inferno, danced with a newfound grace, her spirit a phoenix rising from the ashes of bondage. He watched the tapestry of history weave time and justice into a delicate fabric. He'd glimpsed Sarah's future, downloaded the raw pain into his implant, and yet, seeing it unfold before him was almost unbearable. He felt a change coming on the horizon.

His neural implant, called the oracle in his time, pulsed with information: weather patterns, patrol routes, and the location of a hidden abolitionist network. Armed with this forbidden knowledge, he became the spectral whisperer, slipping through the cracks of the night, sabotaging patrols, and leaving cryptic messages that fueled the rebels' resolve. However, these were mere ripples compared to the tidal wave raging within him, a yearning to reach out, to shield Sarah from the storm he felt responsible of creating.

One sweltering afternoon, the sound of crickets reached a fever pitch, mirroring the inferno in Sarah's eyes. Silas, finally catching a whiff of the rebellion, unleashed his fury. The whip's cruel song lashed against Sarah's back and countless others, a gruesome melody whose chorus tore at Jason's very sanity. He couldn't let her become another martyr, another face etched in the tapestry of his memories.

Night came. From a time far ahead, Jason's shoes whispered ever so faintly against the earth as he navigated the terrain. A detailed map was imprinted on his neural implant. He knew every shadow, every patrol route, every creak of the floorboards in Blackwood's mansion. Using his knowledge, he led the rebels on a desperate flight, a river of shadows weaving through the cotton fields, pursued by the snarls of hounds, the glint of lanterns and gunshots.

He pushed them on, his heart echoing the thud of Sarah's bare feet against the earth. There was a spark in her eyes, a fierceness that resonated with his desperation. He saw his responsibility mirrored in her gaze, the burden of knowledge shared across the abyss of time.

Finally, a rumble split the night, a wagon emerged from the North like a beacon of hope. He tipped off the abolitionist network, his coded messages finding sanctuary in the rustling leaves and chirping crickets. He negotiated with the men of the network. Sarah was to go with them around midnight. That night was special; Sarah was to be freed. She boarded the wagon of the abolitionists, her hand lingering for a fleeting moment on his outstretched arm. She had been delivered to freedom by her descendant.

The wagon creaked away, carrying the fire embers, the seeds of a future Jason had nurtured in the fertile ground of defiance. He stood alone, watching it disappear into the horizon, a silent sentinel in the storm's wake. The battle for Sarah, for freedom itself, wasn't over. It was just the beginning of a long, perilous dance, a waltz between revolution and annihilation.

He turned back toward Meadowbrook, the weight of his responsibility settling on his shoulders. He had played his part, but the internal conflict within Blackwood remained. Now, he had to delve deeper and navigate the treacherous currents of betrayal and loyalty swirling within the confines of the plantation. He had to find allies, hidden levers of influence, anything to weaken Blackwood's hold and pave the way for a future where Sarah and others like her could author their own story, unburdened by the chains of the past.

The clock was ticking, and the echoes of freedom, amplified by Sarah's escape, had become a deafening roar. Jason had to move to orchestrate the next act of this rebellion, a dance played out in the shadows of Blackwood, where his love for Sarah, knowledge of the future, and unwavering courage were his only true weapons.

Chapter 4

Serpents in Eden

Blackwood Plantation was on the brink of dramatic change. The silence was heavy, punctuated only by the creak of wind through the eerie oaks and the hushed whispers of fear that snaked through the slave quarters. This was Jason's chance. However, he walked a tightrope of suspicion and opportunity.

He knew Blackwood was wounded, the escape a festering wound on its pride. Silas, his eyes bloodshot and beard unkempt, limped to and fro like an injured lion, losing its grip on its pride and kingdom. It was the perfect time to plant seeds of discord, to exploit the cracks in the master's house.

His first stop was Thomas, the head carpenter, a man scarred by time and injustice. Drawing from the whispered histories he'd downloaded, Jason spoke of Thomas's ancestors, proud builders who built more than houses – they were the creators of communities for generations. He subtly pointed out the shoddy repairs on the plantation buildings, the warped wood, and buckling foundations, all because of a lack of resources and all hinting at Silas's greed and neglect.

The seed took root. Thomas, his eyes glinting with a flicker of ancestral pride, voiced concern about the safety of the buildings. A chorus of others soon joined. Soon, hushed murmurs about the structural integrity of the buildings and Silas's misplaced priorities became a steady drumming that reached the master's ears.

Next, Jason turned to Mary, the head cook, a woman who wielded flour and fire with equal prowess. He shared stories of forgotten herbs, spices that could bring back long-loss flavors, and dishes fit for kings. He encouraged her to experiment, push the boundaries of the meager rations, and remind everyone, including

Silas, of the hidden wealth they possessed right under their noses.

Mary's culinary revolution was a silent rebellion. The aromas of exotic spices, the whispers of forgotten delicacies, wafted through the air, a compelling reminder of freedom and self-worth. These were reminders of a stolen legacy. Lured by the promise of newfound culinary prestige, Silas grudgingly approved her experiments, oblivious to the seeds of defiance emanating from every sip and nibble.

Within Blackwood, not all snakes lay dormant. Mr. Higgins, the overseer, a man whose cruelty was etched in the lines of his face, watched Jason with suspicion. He witnessed how Jason's words stirred discontent and how his silence held secrets deeper than any future gadget. Higgins knew he was a viper at the feet of Blackwood, poised to strike.

One moonless night, Higgins cornered Jason in the stables, the stench of hay and fear heavy in the air. "What game are you playing, boy?" he snarled, his voice a rusty blade. "You stir up trouble with the slaves; whisper promises you can't keep. What benefit do you reap from their misery?"

Jason met his gaze with a chilling smile. "Perhaps," he said, his voice low and dangerous, "I see a future where the serpents of Blackwood find themselves coiling around their masters."

The threat hung heavy in the air, a declaration of war disguised as a prophecy. Higgins, fear etching new lines on his face, stumbled back. He understood the veiled challenge, the game Jason was playing in the shadows. This was no future teller, a serpent in disguise, hissing vengeance through the echoes of time.

As dawn painted the sky with a murky gold, Jason emerged from the stables, the weight of his secrets heavier than ever. He ignited the embers of dissent, but the fire still simmered, uncertain of its future direction. He had to fan the flames, find an ally within Blackwood itself, someone who could strike a blow from the inside, someone like... Miss Amelia is the frail yet fiercely independent daughter of Silas.

Miss Amelia, too, held secrets, a quiet rebellion brewing in her refusal to conform, her fascination with the forbidden tales of abolitionists and freedom. In her fragile defiance, Jason saw a potential weapon, a pawn in his intricate game of shadows. He knew the risks, the danger of manipulating another for his cause, but the memory of Sarah's fiery eyes fueled his resolve.

The battle for Blackwood, for Sarah, for a future unshackled by the chains of the past, had begun and set to intensify. Jason, the serpent in a garden of immorality and injustice, was ready to play his deadliest hand.

Chapter 5

Whispers and Smoke

Miss Amelia Blackwood was a paradox wrapped in lace and secrets. Fragile as a porcelain doll, her eyes held a glint of tempered steel. Jason approached her with the delicate tread of a Cossack on a frozen river in winter. One wrong move and the entire game could shatter around him. He located her in the garden, surrounded by jasmine blooms that mimicked the pale fragility of her skin. He presented himself as the enigmatic future-teller, weaving tales of advancements and hidden wonders, subtly sowing seeds of doubt about the South's stagnant progress and Blackwood's precarious future.

Amelia listened, her curiosity masked by a veil of polite indifference. Jason, now trained in the subtleties of human interaction from the implant, saw the flicker of rebellion in her eyes, the way her fingers curled into fists when he mentioned the injustice of slave labor. In her, he saw a kindred spirit, a yearning for a different future trapped within the gilded cage of her birthright.

He left coded messages hidden in the pages of forbidden novels she borrowed from his "futuristic library," cryptic prophecies hinting at a world where cotton fields didn't bleed and women possessed minds and dreams beyond the boundaries of marriage and motherhood. Amelia devoured these messages, her eyes sparkling with a dangerous glint as she deciphered the veiled whispers of a future where she could be more than a porcelain ornament to be placed on the Blackwood mantle.

Meanwhile, the serpents he'd awakened within Blackwood continued to writhe. Thomas, fueled by pride in his ancestors' legacy, protested silently, refusing to fix the dilapidated buildings until Silas addressed the shoddy materials and dangerous conditions. Emboldened by the whispers of culinary freedom, Mary refused to serve Silas his usual bland fare, replacing it with dishes bursting with forgotten flavors and hidden messages of defiance.

The tension within Blackwood simmered, reaching a boiling point in the sweltering heat of the Southern summer. Silas, his paranoia gnawing at his already frayed sanity, accused Jason of witchcraft, his booming voice echoing through the halls. Jason, calm as a serpent coiled and ready to strike, met his accusations with veiled threats and cryptic pronouncements of impending upheaval.

A fire razed Blackwood's stables that night, the flames dancing in the darkness like a defiant omen. Whispers blamed slaves, but Jason knew better. He had subtly manipulated Mr. Higgins' fear, playing on his paranoia and turning him into a pawn in his own game. The fire, a controlled chaos, was a message – Blackwood was vulnerable, its foundations rotten from within.

As the smoke of the fire cleared, Amelia approached Jason, her eyes brimming with a dangerous mix of excitement and fear. "Is this... your future?" she asked, her voice barely a whisper.

Jason looked into her eyes, seeing his desperation reflected at him. "This is," he said, his voice low and laced with conviction, "a future we can choose if we are brave enough to reach for it."

The die was cast. The serpent struck, and now he and Amelia had to face the consequences of their gamble. The dance of shadows had reached its crescendo, and the fate of Blackwood, and perhaps of Sarah, hung in the balance.

Chapter 6

Ashes and Embers

The morning sun cast long, accusing shadows across the still-smoldering remains of Blackwood's stables. The air hung heavy with the smokey scent of wood and betrayal. Fear, like a creeping vine, tightened its grip on the hearts of the inhabitants. Like a silent sentinel amidst the chaos, Jason felt the tension crackling around him, the weight of his gamble pressing down on his soul.

Within the crumbling walls of the master's house, Silas Blackwood raged. His face, contorted in a mask of fury, rivaled the charred timbers in its redness. Mr. Higgins, cowering before his wrath, stammered out accusations of the enslaved people, painting them as pyromaniacs fueled by Jason's "devilish whisperings." But Silas, his paranoia gnawing at the edges of his sanity, found little comfort in these easy scapegoats. He looked towards Jason, suspicion burning in his eyes like embers in the ashes.

Amelia, cloaked in mourning black, stood defiant amidst the turmoil. The fire, born from the whispers of rebellion Jason had planted, had ignited an inferno within her spirit. Gone was the porcelain doll; in her place stood a woman sculpted from the flames of change, a steely resolve replacing the porcelain gleam in her eyes.

Amelia stepped forward as Silas railed, demanding retribution, her voice cutting through the hysteria like a blade through the smoke. "This fire," she declared, her words ringing with newfound power, "was not sparked by slaves but by the rot within these very walls. By the injustice that festers in the cotton fields, by the silent screams of those you oppress."

Her words hung heavy in the air, a challenge that cracked the veneer of Blackwood's authority. Silas,

25

taken aback by his daughter's defiance, sputtered incoherently, his grip on power slipping like grains of sand through his fingers.

Amidst the chaos, Jason observed with a serpent's cold detachment. Amelia's rebellion, once a flickering candle flame, had become a roaring bonfire, illuminating the cracks in the system he had so carefully exploited. The question wasn't whether Blackwood would fall but who would be at the helm when the ashes settled.

The answer arrived sooner than expected. A rumble echoed through the fields from the North, growing louder with each passing moment. It was the sound of freedom carried on the wheels of the abolitionist wagon, the same one that had carried Sarah to safety.

Panic seized Silas. He ordered his men to bar the way, a desperate last stand against the tide of change he had refused to see coming. Before violence could erupt, Amelia stepped forward, once more. She ordered the gates thrown open with a quiet authority that surprised even Jason.

The wagon rumbled through, a venerable Trojan horse filled with hope. Sarah, her eyes blazing with a fire that mirrored the burning stables, stood at the forefront as a symbol of freedom, beckoning the slaves to unshackle themselves and join her. The slaves, emboldened by Amelia's defiance and Sarah's presence, looked upon her with awe and longing. Here, there was a connection amongst people unseen in this age, reminiscent of when humanity took its very first unified steps in Africa.

At that moment, lines were drawn amidst the ashes and embers of the rebellion. Silas stood alone, clinging to the ruins of his power, while the future unfurled before him like a tapestry woven in unfamiliar patterns that whispered of a different world. Jason faded into the shadows, his work done, his gamble won.

A shiver ran down his spine as the wagons disappeared into the horizon, carrying Sarah and the seeds of a new tomorrow. The future, though bright, was far from guaranteed. The fight for freedom for justice was only beginning. And he, the Manipulator, the Whisperer, knew he would have to choose his role in the story yet to be written.

Chapter 7

From Ashes to Dawn

The charred remnants of Blackwood Plantation stood as a grim monument to the past. Once thick with smoke and whispers of rebellion, the air now carried the scent of fresh earth and hesitant hope. The slaves, no longer shackled at their wrists but with questions in their eyes, milled about, uncertain of this new dawn.

Amelia Blackwood, her porcelain facade shattered by the flames, stood amidst the wreckage, a phoenix rising from the ashes of her gilded cage. Once distant and cold, her gaze now held a fierce determination; the embers of defiance fanned into a steady flame.

Jason, the serpent shed of its skin, watched from the shadows. His role as the Creator of Whispers was over. Now, rebuilding, of forging a new future from the ashes of the old, lay not in his hands but in the hands of those he had nudged towards freedom.

He approached Amelia, not with the veiled pronouncements of a future-teller but with the humility of a man who had gambled with lives and witnessed the cost. "What comes next, Amelia?" he asked, his voice raspy with the weight of responsibility.

Amelia turned to him, her gaze unwavering. "We rebuild," she said, her voice a quiet tremor that echoed through the ruins. "We rebuild not just these walls, but our lives, our dignity, our right to a future where the sun shines on us all, not just the privileged few."

The task was daunting. The whispers of freedom had attracted not just the slaves of Blackwood but also others from neighboring plantations, drawn by the scent of change like moths gathering around a flame. The fields, once teeming with the injustice of forced labor, stood silent, the cotton serving as a reminder of the shackles they had just cast off.

Food was scarce, the buildings were dilapidated, and fear was a constant shadow lurking at the edges of their newfound freedom. Within the ashes bloomed a spirit of resilience. The slaves, no longer mere tools, pooled their skills and knowledge, their hands, once bound by chains, now shaping a future brick by brick.

Jason offered his strength and ingenuity. He taught the people the forgotten crop rotation techniques, helped build makeshift shelters, and shared his knowledge of basic medicine, a legacy from his own time. These measures helped make the transition easier.

His relationship with Amelia evolved. No longer the veiled manipulator, he became her confidante, her sounding board. They argued, strategized, and dreamed together, their voices weaving a tapestry of hope against the backdrop of a world still shrouded in prejudice.

The world beyond Blackwood was a different story. The fire that had consumed the stables had ignited a spark of rebellion, but it had also attracted the attention of the authorities. Silas Blackwood, his pride bruised, and his wealth diminished, sought revenge, his accusations of arson and treason echoing through the courts.

News of the escaped slaves reached the North, stirring abolitionist networks and igniting a firestorm of debate. The future, once a whispered promise, became a battleground, the struggle for equality spilling beyond the confines of Blackwood and into the larger canvas of a nation divided.

As the sun dipped below the horizon, casting long shadows across the rebuilding fields, Jason and Amelia stood side by side, two figures silhouetted against the embers of a new dawn. The journey ahead was fraught with danger, the scars of the past still fresh, but in their eyes, even as the shadows lengthened, burned a flicker of defiance, a promise whispered on the wind: "We rebuild. We fight. We will not be broken."

Chapter 8

Whispers in the Ashes

The moon cast a spectral glow over the ramshackle shelters that now dotted the once well-kept lawns of Blackwood. The air hummed with the rhythmic thrum of crickets and the murmured anxieties of a community still reviving itself. Jason navigated the makeshift lanes like a firefly amidst the shadows, his gaze drawn to Amelia's silhouette atop the manor house's charred remains.

She walked out on the splintered balcony. The weight of responsibility etched new lines on her once-porcelain face, lines mirrored in Jason's reflection as he reached her side.

"They're calling it the Blackwood Rebellion," Amelia said, her voice a hushed echo against the canvas of the night. "Silas is rabid, spitting vitriol and accusations like a cornered viper."

Jason leaned against the warped balustrade, the creak of a lament from the fallen mansion. "He won't win," he said, his words laced with the quiet certainty of the future he'd glimpsed. "This fire, Amelia, it's ignited a spark that can't be extinguished."

In her eyes, he saw a flicker of doubt, a fear that stretched beyond the immediate threats of Silas' venomous accusations. It was the fear of the unknown, of a future still shrouded in the uncertainty of their rebellion.

He reached out, his hand brushing against hers, a hesitant touch against the rough wood of the railing. The act, small as it was, resonated with unspoken understanding. He, too, harbored fears, the burden of his knowledge a double-edged sword. He could glimpse the potential triumphs and the treacherous shadows that lurked on the path ahead.

As the moon sank lower, casting long, skeletal shadows across the fields, they spoke not of tactics or strategies but of dreams. He shared stories of his own time, of towering cities that kissed the clouds and machines that spun dreams into reality. She painted a future rooted in the fertile soil of Blackwood, where cotton bloomed not as a symbol of oppression but as a testament to their hard-won freedom.

Their voices, weaving past, present, and future through the night, became a tapestry of hope, an unspoken pact forged in the crucible of shared vulnerability. Feeling more at home in this world, Jason found solace in her resilience, a grounding force in the chaos of his own displaced existence. Sarah, the porcelain doll, shattered and restored, saw in him a reflection of her yearning for a world beyond the gilded cage of her birth.

The night wore on, the stars shimmering like watchful eyes above. As the first hint of dawn kissed the horizon, painting the sky in hues of lavender and rose, they descended from their perch, a shared resolve hardening in their gaze. The whispers of the night transformed into a silent vow, a promise etched in the ashes of Blackwood: they would face the world together, the serpent and the phoenix, hand in hand, their defiance a beacon against the encroaching darkness.

Chapter 9

Serpents in the Courtroom

The air in the town square crackled with a tension thicker than summer heat. Whispers of the Blackwood Rebellion danced on the wind, carried from field hand to merchant, slave to magistrate. Jason shrouded in his usual cloak of anonymity, felt the tremors beneath the cobblestones, the simmering fear threatening to boil over.

Silas Blackwood, a gaunt specter fueled by vengeance and bitterness, stalked the courtroom like a caged lion. His accusations, hurling his venom of scorn and retribution, painted Jason as a diabolical manipulator, the serpent who tempted Eve in the Garden of Blackwood.

"He poisoned their minds with tales of a future that doesn't belong to them," Silas roared, his voice echoing through the rafters. "He stirred their discontent, fanned the flames of rebellion, and used my daughter as a pawn in his devilish game!"

Poised and defiant, Amelia stood beside Jason, her porcelain facade replaced by the tempered steel of a warrior. Her unwavering and clear gaze met Silas' with a challenge that crackled in the air. He saw no weakness in her eyes but a phoenix born from the ashes of his arrogance.

The proceedings were a sham, a charade orchestrated by Silas and his ilk to reclaim control, to extinguish the spark of defiance that still smoldered in the hearts of the freed slaves. Yet, Jason knew they couldn't simply stand by and be devoured by this unjust malarkey.

His knowledge of the future, a weapon honed in the shadows, became his shield in the courtroom. He countered Silas' accusations with subtle truths, veiled prophecies that hinted at the injustices woven into the very fabric of their society. He painted a picture of a world where cotton wasn't the blood of their labor but a symbol of their resilience, a future where Black people didn't just till the fields but sculpted destinies beyond the shackles of bondage.

His words, whispered as if carried on the wings of a future breeze, found resonance in the jury's hearts, men and women whose own lives were stained by the injustices he subtly unveiled. Long tipped in favor of the powerful, the scales of justice trembled.

Silas, sensing the shift, unleashed a final impromptu salvo of accusations. He presented forged papers fabricated evidence woven from the twisted threads of his imagination, painting Jason as an agent of a northern conspiracy and a harbinger of chaos and bloodshed.

The tension in the courtroom became a suffocating, ominous pressure of the all-encompassing type that constricted throats and quickened breaths. Even Amelia faltered for a moment, doubt clouding her eyes. There seemed to be only one verdict in this grand finale, where the status quo loomed larger than ever in its desire to persist.

Jason remained calm as if a serpent lying in wait. He met Silas' gaze, a distant gleam in his eyes, and with a voice laced with the certainty of the future he'd glimpsed, declared, "The truth, like freedom, cannot be imprisoned by forged whispers and manufactured shadows. It will prevail, just as surely as the sun rises tomorrow."

His words hung heavy in the air, a challenge resonating with the jury, a spark of hope amidst the suffocating smoke of doubt. The fate of the rebellion, of Jason and Amelia, hung in the precarious balance of the jury's deliberation, a battleground not of muskets and cannons but of whispers and shadows, where the fight for freedom would be decided not on the battlefield, but in the hearts and minds of men.

Chapter 10

Scales of Justice in the Balance

T he jury room, a cramped box echoing with the weight of uncertainty, became a microcosm of the nation, torn between the shackles of the past and the flickering torch of change. Each member grappled with truths and whispered through the veil of time.

James, the old farmer, his hands gnarled from years of tilling unforgiving soil, saw in Jason's words a reflection of his yearning for a future where his children wouldn't inherit the yoke of servitude. Yet, the shadow of Silas' accusations, painted with the vivid hues of fear and reprisal, clung to him like a stubborn weed that refused to be uprooted.

Mary, the stoic seamstress, her fingers nimble from stitching, felt the echoes of forgotten dreams resonate in Jason's prophecies. Visions of a world where her skills weren't confined to mending the frayed edges of another's existence but used to weave tapestries of her destiny flickered in her mind while battling the fear of the unknown.

Young Thomas, the apprentice printer, his eyes ablaze with the rebellious spirit of youth, saw in Jason a kindred spirit, a champion of a future where knowledge wasn't the privileged whisper of the few but a song sung by all. Yet, the whispers of doubt, sown by Silas' venom, gnawed at the edges of his conviction, threatening to extinguish the flickering flame of hope.

Jason moved through the room, painting pictures of possibilities. He planted seeds of discontent, not by decrying the present but by subtly unveiling the beauty of a different tomorrow. He spoke of inventions, machines that could ease the burden of labor, and schools where minds, not just fields, were cultivated.

He wove stories of Black farmers who owned their land, children who learned to read and write, and lives no longer defined by the color of one's skin but by the dreams one dared to chase. He painted a future where cotton wasn't just a symbol of oppression but a testament to their hard-won dignity. In this future, the scales of justice, long tipped in favor of the powerful, hung in perfect balance, available for all to savor.

Sitting across from Jason on the edge of the cliff of change, Amelia watched the jury wrestle with their demons. Her faith in Jason, forged in the rebellion's crucible, remained unwavering, but she saw the fear, prejudice, and deeply ingrained doubts clouding their minds.

The room became a battleground, not of fists and cannons, but of whispers and nightmares. Silas' accusations, like poisonous fangs, sank deep, leaving festering wounds of doubt. Like fragile butterfly wings, Jason's prophecies offered hope, but the slightest tremor of fear could crush their delicate beauty.

As the sun dipped below the horizon, casting long shadows across the courtroom, the jury reached a stalemate. Justice, perched on the scales, held her breath, awaiting the verdict that would decide not just the fate of Jason but also the fragile spark of freedom ignited in the ashes of Blackwood.

Chapter 11

Dawn Breaks in Uncertain Hues

Once abuzz with the malicious whispers of accusations and the nervous murmurs of speculation, the courthouse hall now stood shrouded in suffocating silence. The jury's deliberation, a locked box holding the fate of not just Jason and Amelia but the fledgling hope of freedom birthed from the ashes of Blackwood, stretched into an eternity punctuated only by the frantic ticking of the grandfather clock.

Jason paced back and forth like a caged panther, his movements restless but purposeful. The future, once a tapestry woven with the confidence of his knowledge, now blurred at the edges, the threads threatened by the insidious shadows of uncertainty. He stole glances at Amelia, her porcelain frame seemingly fragile beneath the weight of the situation, yet as always, her defiance was seen burning brightly and firmly in her eyes.

They spoke in stolen moments, whispers against the backdrop of silence. He shared fragmented glimpses of alternate futures, verdicts swinging on the whim of chance, and paths twisting and turning, each leading to a different tomorrow. Amelia, her voice steady despite the tremor in her fingers, reminded him of their journey, the community they had nurtured from the ruins, and the dreams they had dared to build brick by agonizing brick.

Their bond, forged in the crucible of rebellion, deepened in those stolen moments. He saw not just the phoenix reborn from the ashes but the woman beneath, the unwavering heart, the unyielding spirit that mirrored his own. She saw not just the serpent who whispered of futures unseen but the man who stood beside her, vulnerable yet resolute, his belief in their cause unwavering.

As the moon climbed higher, painting the night sky in shades of silver and indigo, they found solace in each other's presence. They shared stories, memories, and hopes, weaving a tapestry of defiance against the looming shadows. He described the dazzling lights of his time, the soaring towers that kissed the clouds, the machines that spun dreams into reality. She spoke of Blackwood's fertile soil, of fields yielding not just cotton but a future nurtured by their own hands where those who once worked the fields might be masters.

Their world, previously confined by the courtroom's walls, expanded through the whispers of their dreams. They envisioned a future where children of all colors learned in the same schools, fields sang with laughter instead of echoing with cries of pain, and justice hung true on the scales, unburdened by the weight of prejudice.

The dream was fragile, its edges frayed by the uncertainty gnawing at their hearts. Each tick of the clock was a hammer blow against their hope, a stark reminder of the precariousness of their situation. The sun, they knew, would rise, but whether it would illuminate a dawn of freedom or set in despair and defeat remained agonizingly unclear.

The courtroom door creaked open as the first rays of dawn painted the horizon in fiery hues. The jury, their faces hung with the weight of their decision, filed in, silence clinging to them like a shroud. Amelia and Jason intertwined like vine and oak, their breaths held in shared anticipation, and turned to face their fate.

With the judge's gavel pounding against the hardened wood, there was not just the clang of finality but the echo of a future yet written. As the words "Not guilty" reverberated through the hall, a collective sigh of relief washed over the room. In that fragile moment, the scales of justice had tipped toward hope, their victory a small step on the long road to freedom.

Amelia and Jason knew this was just the beginning. The scars of their rebellion, like the charred remnants of Blackwood, would linger. The serpent and the phoenix, forever bound by their shared defiance, would have to navigate the treacherous path ahead, hand in hand, their dreams a flickering torch against the lingering shadows of the past.

Chapter 12

Echoes of Freedom in the Ashes

The jubilation outside the courthouse was a cacophony of stomping feet, raised voices, and laughter choked with tears. The freed slaves, a sea of faces etched with hope and disbelief, danced to the rhythm of a future finally within reach. Sarah, her eyes blazing with a fire that mirrored the setting sun, led the cheers, her voice hoarse but unyielding.

Amelia, cloaked in the golden light of freedom, stood hand in hand with Jason amid the revelry. The weight of uncertainty had lifted, replaced by a cautious optimism. The past, a smoldering ruin, still cast long shadows, but the phoenix within her soared, wings catching the scent of possibilities.

Silas Blackwood sat alone inside the courtroom, a solitary statue carved into pure bitterness. The verdict, a death blow to his pride and power, echoed in the hollow chambers of his heart. His fury, a caged beast, roared within him, gnashing its teeth at the injustice of it all. His plans, meticulously crafted with venomous whispers and forged documents, had crumbled. The slaves, once mere tools, now stood defiant, their freedom a mocking echo in the gilded halls of his fallen kingdom. Yet, even in his ruin, a chilling ember of malice flickered in his eyes. He would not be easily defeated.

Back in Blackwood, rebuilding began. The charred remnants of the manor house, a grim monument to the past, were a stark reminder of the battle they had won and the challenges ahead. Once silent with forced labor, the fields buzzed with activity as families carved out their own plots, hope blossoming amidst the scorched earth.

Jason rolled his sleeves, grabbed a dusty shovel, and joined the work. He taught them futuristic and exotic techniques for ensuring bountiful crops, helped build makeshift shelters, and shared his knowledge of basic medicine and inoculation, a legacy from his own time. His gift, he realized, lay not in whispering prophecies but in offering the tools to help these people forge their future.

Amelia emerged as a natural leader, like the phoenix from the ashes. She organized the community, settled disputes, and nurtured the embers of hope into a steady flame. Her voice, no longer a porcelain whisper, rang with authority and compassion, a beacon guiding them through the labyrinth of uncertainty.

Though filled with the sweat of labor and the gnaw of hunger, the days were imbued with a newfound joy. Children, no longer burdened by the chains of servitude, played amongst the cotton stalks, their laughter a song of freedom echoing through the reborn fields. Elders, their backs bent with years of toil, shared stories of a past endured and a future glimpsed, their eyes reflecting the flickering flames of hope.

The world beyond Blackwood remained a storm cloud on the horizon. Silas, wounded and vengeful, plotted his next move. Whispers of retribution, carried on the wings of fear, reached the ears of the community. The threat of reprisal, enemies lurking in the shadows, cast doubt over their fragile triumph.

Amelia, aware of the dangers that lie in wait, gathered the freed slaves under the skeletal remains of the manor house. Though laced with the awareness of perils ahead, her voice remained resolute. "Freedom," she declared, her gaze sweeping across the faces of hope and apprehension, "is not a gift, but a battle won, and a battle earned. We must remain vigilant, united, and watchful of the shadows that still seek to dim our light."

Blackwood stood at a crossroads. The ashes of the past still smoldered, but from them, a fragile phoenix had risen. Jason stood beside it, a silent guardian offering his knowledge and strength. Amelia led the way, her eyes fixed on the horizon, where the sun of a new dawn, though obscured by uncertainty, beckoned them onward.

Chapter 13

Whispers Across the Wires

The flickering flames of a kerosene lamp cast long shadows across Jason's face as he hunched over a makeshift workbench in the heart of Blackwood. Tools scavenged from abandoned workshops, and scraps of metal salvaged from the wreckage of the past lay scattered around him. His hands now moved with the practiced dexterity of the best engineer of his time.

He was building not just shelters or tools but also a weapon against the very chains that bound the nation in the grip of slavery. His whispers, once woven in secret courts and smoke-filled rooms, now flowed through a different conduit - wires twisted together like the threads of destiny, cobbled from scraps of future technology. His solar-powered implant guided his every move.

His mind, adrift in the vast ocean of his knowledge, dredged up memories of ancient inventions in his time: printing presses churning out words like ammunition, telegraph wires singing rebel songs across the land. Adapting these ghosts of future progress to the present, he fashioned crude transmitters and receivers, weaving a makeshift communication network between Blackwood and the nascent flames of abolitionist fervor beyond the horizon.

Amelia stood beside him, her gaze mirroring the spark of revolution in his eyes. "Do you truly believe it will work?" she asked, her voice a hushed tremor in the quiet night.

"Hope," Jason replied, his voice laced with the certainty of a future he had glimpsed, "is a fragile thing, Amelia. But nurtured by the right tools, it can ignite a wildfire."

Months passed before the system was up and running. The first message, encoded in a series of flickering lamp signals, was simple: "Blackwood stands free." It danced across the wires, a spark leaping from field to town, from church basement to the abolitionist meetings, painting the night sky with the faint luminescence of shared defiance.

In the North, the embers of resistance, stirred by whispers of the Blackwood Rebellion, grew into a crackling fire. Underground presses, fueled by Jason's smuggled pamphlets and news clippings, churned out stories of the taste of freedom and broken shackles. Armed with knowledge of future events gleaned from Jason's cryptic pronouncements, Abolitionist leaders maneuvered the political chessboard like seasoned masters.

The South seethed. Silas Blackwood rallied his ilk, painting Jason as a devil, whispering lies, and inciting bloodshed. Politicians, their pockets lined with cotton profits, branded Blackwood a festering wound that needed cleansing. The press, a puppet whose strings were controlled by the powers that be, spewed vitriol and veiled threats, casting the fledgling community in the harshest of lights.

The tension crackled across the nation, a spark waiting for the wind. Jason knew the storm was coming. He had ignited a fire, but its warmth wouldn't reach every corner unless he fanned it with the full force of the tools at his disposal.

He scrounged for more materials, pushing the limits of his makeshift technology. He built projectors, flickering ghosts of future wonders that displayed images of a world without slavery, children learning together, and fields yielding bounty for all. He constructed rudimentary loudspeakers, amplifying the voices of escaped slaves, their stories of suffering and resilience echoing through the streets of cities far from Blackwood.

The backlash was swift and brutal. Bounty hunters, spurred by promises of gold and fueled by hate, descended upon Blackwood. Silas plotted to crush the rebellion and silence the serpent forever. In the North, political forces, threatened by the rising tide of change, sought to extinguish the flames before they devoured the nation.

Yet, amid the storm, the whispers on the wires continued. Stories of Blackwood's resistance, amplified by Jason's ingenuity, sparked copycat rebellions across the South. Slaves, emboldened by the example of Blackwood, rose in whispers and roars, their chains rattling like a death knell for the old order.

Jason and Amelia, the serpent, and the phoenix, stood at the forefront of the storm. They rallied their community, trained them in the martial arts of his era, and armed them with knowledge gleaned from whispers of the future. They became beacons of hope, guiding the winds of change, their defiance a shimmering banner in the gathering's face darkness.

Chapter 14

Whispers Turn to Roars

The South crackled with the heat of rebellion. Jason's whispers on the wires carried on the wings of the wind, and the echoes of hope sparked fires that defied suppression. Across cotton fields and tobacco plantations, the seeds of defiance planted long ago burst into furious and decadent bloom.

In Georgia, under the moss-draped boughs of ancient oaks, a band of runaway slaves, armed with salvaged tools and sharpened machetes, stormed the gates of a notorious plantation. Their leader, a young woman named Maya, her eyes blazing with a fire stoked by Jason's smuggled pamphlets, led the charge with a fury born of generations of stolen lives. The overseer, a bloated caricature of cruelty, fell to her blade, his scream swallowed by the rising tide of freedom chants.

In Virginia, the whispers reached the ears of Jacob, a wizened field hand whose stories of the North, gleaned from Jason's flickering projector images, had fanned the embers of dissent within him. He led a clandestine exodus under the cloak of a moonless night, guiding men, women, and children through hidden paths and whispering valleys. The hounds of the patrollers bayed at their heels, but the taste of freedom spurred them on, their exodus a silent testament to the yearning for a life beyond the lash.

In the shadow of New Orleans, a network of dockworkers and artisans, awakened by smuggled newspapers filled with visions of a future where their skills were valued not for toil but for progress, plotted their defiance. Led by Etienne, a blacksmith whose dreams of crafting wonders instead of shackles mirrored Jason's prophecies, they planned to cripple the city's port, the lifeblood of the slave trade.

The South stirred in its sleep. The whispers on the wires, amplified by Jason's makeshift projectors and loudspeakers, echoed through slave quarters, igniting sparks of rebellion in hearts hardened by years of oppression. Long choked by fear, songs of freedom rose from cotton fields and echoed through shadowed streets, a collective voice rising against the injustices that had stained the land for too long.

Silas Blackwood remained unyielding. His agents, serpents slithering through the shadows, infiltrated rebel ranks, sowing seeds of discord and mistrust. Politicians, their pockets lined with blood-soaked cotton, unleashed a torrent of propaganda, branding the rebellions as acts of barbarity, painting Jason as a demonic mastermind orchestrating chaos from his secluded haven.

The backlash was swift and brutal. Troops, their faces masks of cold indifference, descended upon the nascent flames of rebellion, guns spitting hot lead and fear. Maya, her defiance etched in blood, fell defending her liberated plantation, her sacrifice a torch passed to the hands of countless others. Jacob's exodus, ambushed in a hidden valley, turned into a massacre, the dreams of freedom choked in the smoke of gunfire.

Yet, even in defeat, the whispers on the wires refused to be silenced. New voices rose, taking the place of those fallen. Etienne, his forge crackling with the fury of resistance, led a successful sabotage of the New Orleans port, crippling the slave trade for a crucial week, a defiant thorn in the side of the oppressive machine.

Blackwood stood as a beacon amid the storm, a testament to the enduring spirit of defiance. Jason rallied the survivors, their wounds raw but their resolve unshaken. Amelia, the phoenix rising from the ashes, led them to mourn the fallen and strategize for the future.

The South, though scarred by the backlash, remained restless. The seeds of rebellion, once planted, refused to be easily uprooted. Though carrying tales of loss and fear, the whispers on the wires also echoed with the promise of a future where chains would be broken and shackles cast aside. Jason, the serpent, and the strategist, knew the fight was far from over. Though flickering, the whispers had morphed into roars, and the flames of rebellion would not be extinguished until the South, in all its entirety, tasted the sweet nectar of freedom.

Chapter 15

Shadows in the Cotton Fields

T he whispers on the wires, once a melody of hope, had devolved into a dirge of mourning. The plantation of Oakwood, ablaze with a rebellion just weeks ago, now stood shrouded in a desolate silence. The charred remnants of cabins, skeletal monuments to lost dreams, bore witness to the brutal efficiency of the South's reprisal.

A pall of doubt hung heavier among the survivors than the Mississippi dew. Sarah, eyes haunted by the screams that still echoed in her ears, struggled with the gnawing suspicion that their uprising had been orchestrated only to be crushed. Was Jason, the whisperer from the North, a beacon, or a betrayer? Had their trust and sacrifices been nothing more than fuel for a fire destined to scorch and leave nothing but ashes?

Her doubts resonated with others. Daniel, a young field hand whose youthful bravado had fueled the initial charge, now nursed a festering wound of disillusionment. His hands, once eager to wield shovels as weapons, now trembled with uncertainty, the image of his fallen brother etched forever in his mind. Was their rebellion merely a pawn in a game played by others, far removed from the blood and dust of the cotton fields?

The seed of dissent, planted by whispers of betrayal, flourished in the fertile ground of despair. Whispered accusations slithered through the ranks, venomous snakes slithering through the fragile fabric of their unity. Fingers were pointed, blame traded, the enemy within as insidious as the one without.

Amelia, the phoenix ever aloft, watched the shadows engulf Blackwood with heavy eyes. The weight of leadership, once a mantle of defiance, now felt like a leaden cloak. She saw the doubt festering in Sarah's eyes, the bitterness twisting Daniel's spirit, and knew that the battle for freedom was not waged solely against guns and whips but against the demons that crept in through the cracks of hope.

She gathered them around the smoldering remains of a cabin, the embers of resilience glowing faintly against the encroaching darkness. Her voice, though heavy with grief, remained unwavering. "Betrayal," she said, slicing through the thick air, "can wound as deeply as any cannon. But let not its venom turn us against each other, for that is the true victory our enemies crave."

She shared stories of whispers from the future, not glorious triumphs but the slow, arduous climb towards freedom. Of battles lost and won, of doubt and despair, and of the enduring spirit that kept the embers of hope flickering even in the coldest winds.

Jason stood beside her. His words, once veiled in prophecies, were now raw and honest. He admitted to mistakes, blind spots, and the limitations of his knowledge. He offered no solutions but a shared burden, a hand extended in the darkness.

The firelight danced in Sarah's eyes, her anger morphing into a flicker of understanding. His gaze fixed on the flames; Daniel felt the bitterness ebb, replaced by the embers of his brother's spirit urging him to fight on.

The shadows still lingered, their whispers insidious in the quiet air. Within the circle of flickering firelight, the cracks in their unity mended. The song of freedom, though battered, rose again, a hesitant hymn against the oppressive symphony of the South.

Blackwood, in its desolation, became a crucible. The fire that had consumed them had also forged a resolve, a testament to the fact that even in the ashes of betrayal, the embers of hope could be rekindled. For the war for freedom was not just against an external enemy but against the demons that lurked within, ready to extinguish the fire at its most vulnerable hour.

Chapter 16

Shadows Dance on the Map

The flickering lamplight bathed Blackwood in an amber glow, casting long shadows on the makeshift war room carved from the gutted manor house. Amelia and Jason, two halves of a revolution forged in the fires of defiance, hunched over a crude map etched onto worn parchment. The whispers on the wires, once a battle cry, had become hushed reports of scattered rebellions, each a spark struggling to ignite the tinderbox of the South.

Their task now, etched in the lines on their faces and the gnawing worry in their eyes, was to fan those sparks into a raging inferno. The South had marshaled its might. Troops patrolled the roads, their boots heavy with the threat of reprisal. Plantation owners, eyes glinting with cold fury, tightened their grip on their human chattel. The political tides, once nudged by whispers of reform, had turned viciously against them, branding Jason a subversive and Blackwood a festering wound on the nation's body.

"Direct assaults are out," Amelia stated, her steady voice gripping their situation's chaos. "They'll crush us one by one, a game of gradual and painful elimination across the South."

Jason traced the map with a calloused finger. "We need to shift the ground," he murmured, his gaze fixed on the network of dotted lines representing the telegraph wires. "Weave the rebellions into a tapestry, not isolated pockets."

They spent the night in hushed strategizing, the flickering lamp an audience to their whispered plans. They plotted to leverage the wires, Jason's whispered knowledge of future tactics echoing across the land. They would orchestrate coordinated strikes, not simultaneous, but in quick succession, forcing the

South's forces to dance to their tune, spreading them thin like butter on a too-large slice of bread.

Amelia focused on morale. She knew the whispers on the wires, now carrying news of setbacks and losses, could easily morph into a catastrophe of epic proportions. She planned to send messages of hope and stories of resilience, weaving tales of minor victories and acts of defiance, keeping the fires of rebellion burning even in the darkest corners.

Their strategy, brilliant as it seemed in the lamplight, hinged on a gamble. They needed allies, not just within the South, but in the North, where the winds of political change, though hesitant, were stirring. Jason proposed a daring infiltration mission. He traveled North, disguised, and armed with his knowledge of the future, to sway public opinion and secure critical support for their cause.

Amelia, ever cautious, voiced her concerns. "The North is a viper's nest, Jason. They could turn you over to the South quicker than a blink."

"Then I'll be a viper among vipers," Jason replied, a steely glint in his eyes. "I know their games, Amelia. This is the move we need, the spark that could tip the scales in our favor."

So, under the cloak of a moonless night, Jason vanished. He crossed the Mason-Dixon line, slipping through the cracks, armed with nothing but his wits, his knowledge, and the fragile hope of a nation on his shoulders. Blackwood held its breath, the war room silent except for the crackling fire and Amelia's quiet prayers. The fate of their rebellion, the freedom of a people, now rested on a whispered plan and a serpent venturing into the unknown.

Chapter 17

Echoes of Whispers in the Moonlight

Moonlight this very night was an icy blade slicing through the Mississippi darkness. It bathed the sugarcane fields in an eerie silver glow. Beneath its gaze, a band of figures, cloaked in shadows, armed with salvaged scythes, and sharpened tools, crouched amongst the tall stalks. These were the whispers of Jason's plan, given flesh and bone in the Bayou's Form Runners, a rebel group as elusive as the mists that clung to the riverbanks.

Leading them was Maeve, a woman whose fiery spirit had been tempered by years of hardship. Her eyes, sharp as the crescent moon above, scanned the plantation in the distance, the oppressive bulk of the slave quarters stark against the velvet sky. Tonight, they weren't just fighting for freedom; they were fighting for Sarah, their sister in spirit, abducted by the plantation's overseer, the vile Silas Jr.

The whispers on the wires, Jason's hushed voice from across the Mason-Dixon line, had guided their plan – a coordinated attack timed to coincide with rebellions across the South, to stretch the South's forces thin and create a window of opportunity. Maeve's Bayou Runners, nimble and silent as wraiths, were tasked with a vital distraction - drawing the plantation guards away from the slave quarters long enough for another rebel group, the Delta Hammers, to infiltrate and liberate Sarah.

Maeve raised a hand, the signal passing like a ripple through the tall cane. Each member of the Bayou Runners knew their role; their movements were practiced in the moonlight dances they had used to disguise their drills from prying eyes. One by one, they melted into the shadows, becoming phantoms weaving through the maze of stalks.

A loud cry shattered the night, a carefully staged diversion orchestrated by the Delta Hammers. Maeve and her rag-tag force sprang into action. With the ferocity of cornered wildcats, they materialized at the edges of the plantation, wielding their tools as weapons against the startled guards. Their screams, echoing through the night, served as a rallying cry, effectively drawing the remaining forces away from the slave quarters.

The chaos unfolded like a scene from Jason's whispered prophecies, a coordinated dance of rebellion across the South. Telegraph wires hummed with coded messages, rebellions sparked like scattered flames, and the South's iron grip on its human chattel momentarily faltered.

Amid the triumphant echoes of freedom, doubt gnawed at Maeve's heart. The escape, planned with meticulous precision, felt almost too easy. She had learned the hard way to trust not the moonlit fields but the shadows lurking within them.

Her suspicions proved tragically true. As they neared the slave quarters, they stumbled upon a scene ripped from her worst nightmares. Sarah, her body broken and battered, lay lifeless next to Silas Jr., who grinned at them like a wolf sated on prey. The trap, baited with a staged diversion, had sprung, claiming an innocent life in its cruel jaws.

A wave of grief and rage washed over the Bayou Runners. Fueled by the dream of freedom, their fight turned into a desperate scramble for vengeance. Their tools, meant to cleave sugarcane stalks, sang a different song tonight, a grim aria of retribution.

Silas Jr. met his end on a moonlit blade, his cries swallowed by the triumphant howl of defiance that ripped from Maeve's throat. Yet, the victory tasted like ashes in her mouth. Sarah's face, etched in eternal pain, was a harsh reminder of the price freedom demanded, a price they hadn't factored into Jason's whispers on the wires.

News of the Bayou Runners' success spread like wildfire across the rebel network, tinged with the bitter reality of Sarah's sacrifice. It was a testament to the resilience of the human spirit, a victory born out of tragedy, a flame refusing to be extinguished even in the face of crushing loss.

While the South, enraged by the audacity of the coordinated attacks, launched a ruthless manhunt for the rebels, the whispers on the wires continued. Jason's voice, echoing from the North, carried not just news of the coordinated strikes but also words of caution, of lessons learned in the moonlight fields where hope battled despair.

Tapestries of Freedom

Chapter 18

A Whisper Beyond Time

The air crackled with a different electricity than the telegraph wires used to carry. It was the thrum of despair, a storm cloud hanging heavy over the remnants of the scattered rebellions. Jason stood amidst the ashes, his whispers of revolution now choked by the dust of defeat and losing Sarah.

He had seen glimpses of a future where the South burned in the fires of freedom, but that future belonged to another timeline, one where fate had played its hand differently. Here, in the harsh reality of his present, the South had tightened its grip, its boot stamping out the flames of rebellion one by one.

A gnawing truth, born from whispers beyond the wires, took root in his mind. This fight, confined to the shackles of the present, was doomed to a cyclical dance of bloodshed and despair. Victory, it seemed, could only be found in a different time before the chains were forged before the seeds of hatred were sown.

Over the next few months, he gathered the tattered remnants of the rebellions, their faces etched with the bitter residue of defeat. His voice, no longer a promise of fiery uprisings, was a whisper of a gamble, a leap into the unknown. He spoke of a time before, of Africa untouched by the blight of slavery, of a chance to sever the chain at its very source.

The prospect was met with incredulity, then suspicion, finally flickering into a desperate hope. Was this madness or the last gasp of a dying dream? Jason, his eyes shimmering with the conviction of a prophet, laid out his plan. They would weave a tapestry of time, a bridge made of whispers and stolen glimpses of the past. Together, they would cross the threshold, stepping into the cradle of their stolen history. They would call themselves the warriors of the whirlwind.

The journey was a blur of swirling colors and disorienting sensations. Time, stripped of its linear path, became a malleable river, their makeshift vessel tossed upon its treacherous currents. Fear clawed at their hearts, but the spark of defiance, rekindled by Jason's vision, refused to be extinguished. Jason activated the time machine with Amelia and his thousands of warriors nearby.

They emerged, blinking in the unfamiliar sunlight, in a land untouched by the scars of the future. Lush savannas stretched beneath a vast, unpolluted sky, the air vibrant with the sounds of a world unaware of the chains it would wear. The whispers on the wires, now silent, were replaced by the rhythmic thrumming of djembes and the chanting of ancient stories.

Though met with wary curiosity, their arrival eventually blossomed into a tense understanding. Drawing upon his knowledge of future tactics and diplomacy, Jason navigated the intricate web of tribal politics. He spoke of the future, the horrors that awaited these lands if they remained passive, and the need to forge an alliance against the encroaching darkness.

Initially met with skepticism, his words found fertile ground in the elders' hearts. They saw the ghosts of their future reflected in Jason's stories, the echoes of chains yet to be forged. A treaty was struck, woven from mutual respect and the shared desire for freedom. The tribes of Africa united under the banner of an unspoken prophecy and stood tall against the coming tide of the slave traders.

The battle, when it came, was a clash of epic proportions. Jason's warriors of the whirlwind united with the tribes and fought valiantly. The fighting was intense. Jason, though no warrior, used his knowledge to strategize, his words guiding the tribal leaders in the art of attack and defense. Sun Tzu's art of war was translated and shared orally from village to village. Larn's "The most epic battle strategem," a masterpiece from Jason's time, was shared with the newly formed empires.

Victory, hard-won and stained with blood, finally dawned. The slave traders, defeated and scattered, retreated into the sands, their dreams of plunder turning to bitter ash. Africa, awakened by the whispers of an unwritten future, stood at a crossroads. The chains of slavery, severed at their source, lay broken on the savanna and desert ground.

The fight was far from over. The whispers on the wires had carried echoes of a future where the struggle for freedom continued. Jason and Amelia, standing amidst the triumphant warriors, knew the battle against oppression was a timeless one. Yet, in the eyes of the children playing amongst the fallen weapons, he saw a faint, flickering hope in the joyous celebrations that painted the night sky with laughter. It was a hope not just for Africa but for all who dared to dream of a world without chains, where the whispers of freedom echoed in the wind.

Chapter 19

Whispers into Echoes of Harmony

Time, once a linear path, had become a tangled tapestry. Jason stood amidst the vibrant chaos of a marketplace unlike any he had ever seen. Gone were the shackles, the cowering faces, the oppressive silence. In their place thrummed a symphony of trade, a celebration of unity forged in the crucible of shared adversity.

Here, under the equatorial African sun, representatives from across Sub-Saharan Africa, clad in their ancestral finery, sat alongside envoys from Arab and European states. The whispers in this era, different from Jason's timeline, had evolved into a chorus of diplomacy.

Now a weathered yet visionary figure, Jason had become the architect of this impossible peace. He had used his knowledge of the future not as a weapon but as a map, navigating the treacherous shoals of cultural differences and historical grievances. He had shown them a future where shared prosperity, not exploitation, was the compass guiding their ships.

The treaties, inked on parchment crafted from papyrus and sealed with wax scented with spices from both East and West, were more than just pacts; they were testaments to a new era. Trade routes, once arteries of slavery, now pulsed with the lifeblood of exchange, carrying knowledge, technologies, and spices along their dusty veins.

African scholars flocked to newly established universities, their minds ablaze with the rediscovery of their rich history, severely diminished in Jason's timeline but now reclaimed. Artisans, their talents honed by centuries of tradition, wove intricate textiles, and sculpted gleaming bronze figures; their adorns not just tribal huts but the royal palaces of empires across the globe.

The echoes of the Renaissance, once confined to Europe, resonated across the vast savannas. African architects, drawing inspiration from their heritage and the architectural marvels of their newfound allies, created cities that whispered of ancient wisdom and future possibilities. Once a dusty outpost, Timbuktu blossomed into a beacon of learning, its libraries overflowing with scrolls penned in Arabic, Swahili, Chinese, and European languages, a testament to the power of shared global knowledge.

Jason knew the tapestry of time remained fragile. The threads of prejudice woven into the fabric of history still threatened to unravel this delicate peace. Along with a generation nurtured on the ideals of unity and progress, he stood guard, watchful eyes forever scanning the horizon for the faintest hint of discord. Amelia and the warriors of the whirlwind are forever by his side.

For in the whispers of the wind, carried across the sun-filled savannas, Jason could still hear the faint echoes of chains, a reminder of the battles fought and those yet to come. These whispers were different. They were not echoes of despair but a call to vigilance, a song of a people who had tasted freedom and would not, could not, ever willingly relinquish it.

Chapter 20

Progress Under a Shared Sun

In its keenest sense of artistry, the African sun transformed the marketplace into a mosaic of gold and amber. Once choked by fear, laughter burst out freely, a testament to the fragile victory woven from sacrifice and whispered dreams. Amelia, her gaze tracing through the bustling throngs, spotted Jason. He stood beneath a baobab tree, its gnarled branches reaching towards the sun like ancient, welcoming arms. A young Arab scholar, his eyes bright with intellectual fervor, perched at his side, their conversation a delicate dance of shared knowledge.

Amelia's heart swelled. This was beyond anything they had dreamed of in the flickering lantern light of Blackwood. Here, the chains of the past lay shattered, replaced by a tapestry of unity, where once whispers of rebellion sparked, now bloomed treaties of peace and amity. The air thrummed with the music of trade, merchants from across the desert bartering spices and fabrics, voices weaving a song of progress.

She approached, drawn by the magnetism of their discourse. As she neared, she caught snatches of their conversation: "...irrigation techniques from the Nile...adaptations for drought-resistant crops...knowledge shared, prosperity ensured..." His face animated, Jason gestured toward a field on the horizon, now verdant with life, a stark contrast to the arid plains of his future memories.

The scholar, Ahmed, turned to Amelia, his smile as warm as the desert sun. "He speaks of a future where knowledge, not chains, binds us," he said, his eyes reflecting a shared dream. "He speaks of a time when rivers of learning nourish lands instead of wars."

At that moment, Amelia glimpsed the legacy they had forged. This vibrant marketplace, these children learning beneath the shade of baobab trees, this symphony of progress rising from the ashes of despair was all a testament to their unwavering belief in a future where hope bloomed as wonderfully and colorfully as any tropical flower.

As the sun dipped below the horizon, Jason and Amelia found themselves beneath the baobab, its branches protecting them from the wind.

"Remember the whispers?" Jason asked his voice as soft and sweet as the emerging twilight. "The whispers of chains, of futures stolen?"

Amelia nodded, the bittersweet memory creating a line on her brow. "But those whispers," she said, her voice gaining strength, "they were drowned out by the roar of defiance, by the chorus of a million dreams refusing to be silenced."

They stood in comfortable silence, the echo of their conversation mingling with the chirping crickets and the rustling leaves. An unspoken but understood symbol stood nearby – a broken shackle adorned with vibrant flowers, a stark reminder of the chains they had shattered and the future they had nurtured. Etiene, a seasoned commander in the Warriors of the Whirlwind, created the sculpture.

Under the silent canopy of stars, they reaffirmed their vow in that quiet moment. A vow whispered not from fear but from hope, a promise to keep fanning the flames of progress, to nurture the tapestry of unity, to ensure that the echoes of their struggle would forever resonate in the laughter of children, the wisdom of scholars, and the boundless potential of a world where the largest and most vile enslavement of people never happened.

Chapter 21

Toward a New Future

The year was 1492. Not the one known in history books, but a tapestry woven from whispers, a future salvaged from the flames of despair. In the grand hall of Timbuktu, sunlight filtered through stained glass, casting a kaleidoscope of colors on the assembled dignitaries. The air vibrated with a nervous hum, a prelude to an event destined to echo through the ages.

On one side sat Emperor Sékou Traoré, ruler of the united African Empire, adorned with gold jewelry and royal traditional clothing, his eyes reflecting the wisdom of generations. Opposite him, Sultan Bayezid II, his beard like a snowdrift framing his discerning eyes, represented the Ottoman Empire. His robes, woven with intricate patterns, whispered of ancient power. Beside him, a stern-faced envoy, Rodrigo Mendoza, emissary of Spain, his armor glinting in the stained-glass prism.

The air thrummed with the tension of history in the making. For generations, Africa had known only the sting of exploitation, the chains of slavery a constant reminder of its vulnerability. Today, under the watchful gaze of a new dawn, they were here to rewrite the narrative.

Scribe Ibrahim dipped his quill, the ink glistening like a black teardrop in the sunbeam. With a flourish, he unfurled the parchment, its surface pristine, a blank canvas waiting to be etched with the promise of a future.

Ambassador Mendoza, his voice tinged with formality, stepped forward. He spoke of trade, mutual respect, and a future where spices flowed freely across the oceans. Sultan Bayezid's voice resonant with authority echoed these sentiments, pledging cooperation and an end to the cycle of conflict.

Then came Emperor Traoré. His voice, a deep rumble that resonated in the rafters, spoke of a future where knowledge would be the currency, children from Timbuktu to Toledo would share the same thirst for learning, and the chains of ignorance would be cast aside.

Each phrase, meticulously translated, flowed like molten gold onto the parchment, solidifying into a treaty of peace and amity. A pact not built on fear but on understanding, not forged in the fires of war but in the crucible of shared hope.

As the last strokes were inked, a hush fell over the hall. Emperor Traoré rose, his gaze sweeping across the assembled dignitaries. "Let this day be remembered," he proclaimed, his voice ringing like a clarion call, "not as the end of conflict but as the dawn of a new era. An era where the chorus of shared prosperity shall drown whispers of war and where the future shall sing a song of unity painted in the vibrant hues of freedom and prosperity for all."

The assembled dignitaries rose, their applause echoing through the hall, a thunderous symphony of acceptance of a dream not deferred but unleashed. The warriors of the whirlwind stood up and saluted the Emperor in unison. In that moment, under the sun-drenched Timbuktu sky, Jason, standing amidst the crowd next to

Amelia, felt a warmth bloom in his chest that had nothing to do with the African sun. It was the warmth of victory where millions of whispered dreams were finally given voice, a testament to the indomitable spirit of all mankind.

Dr. William Clifton Green II

www.ingramcontent.com/pod-product-compliance
Lightning Source LLC
Chambersburg PA
CBHW030609130626
46552CB00006B/2703